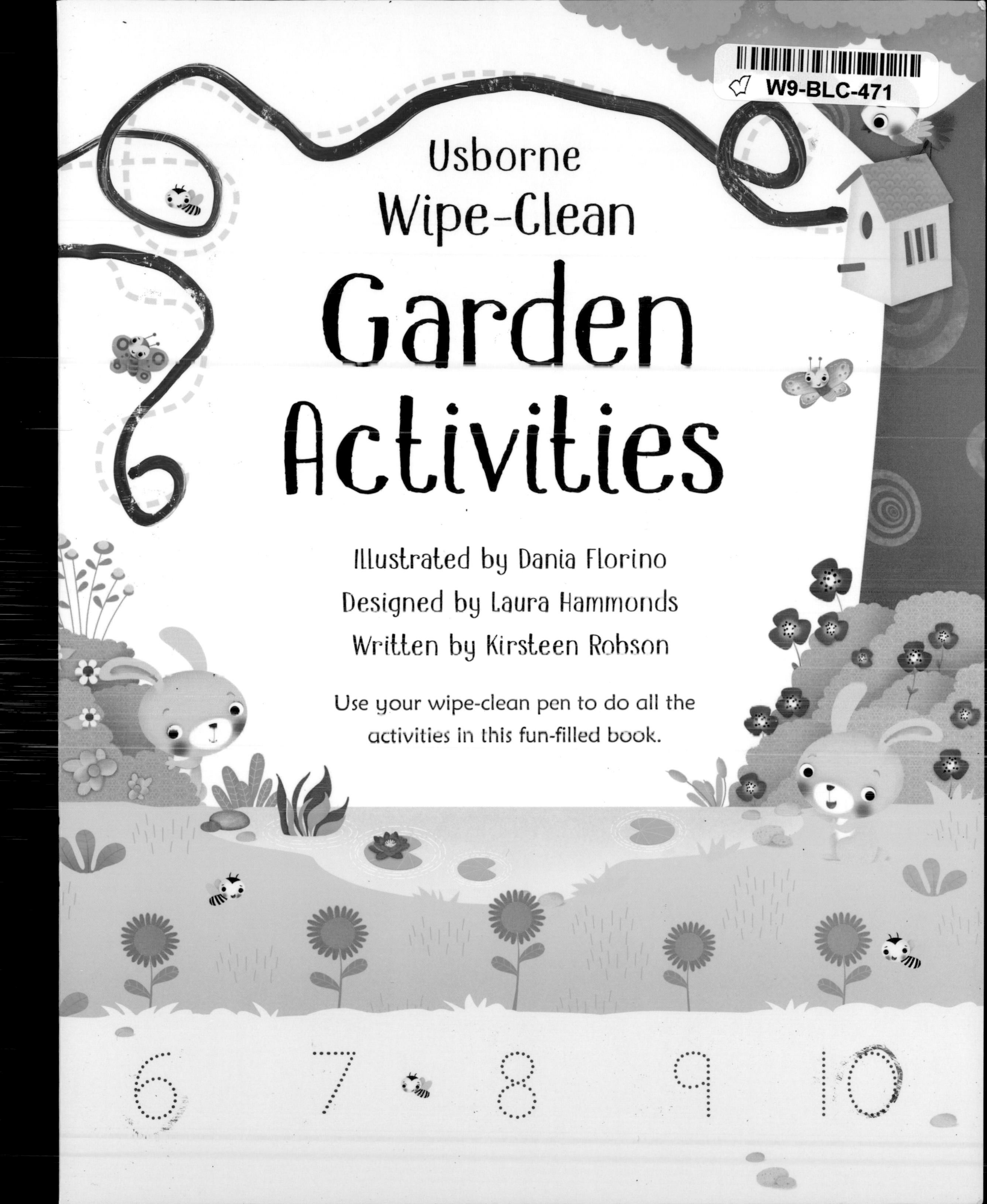

# Usborne Wipe-Clean Garden Activities

Illustrated by Dania Florino

Designed by Laura Hammonds

Written by Kirsteen Robson

Use your wipe-clean pen to do all the activities in this fun-filled book.

# Springtime

Use the pen to draw more leaves on this tree.

Draw over the dots to show Becca Bear where to cut the grass.

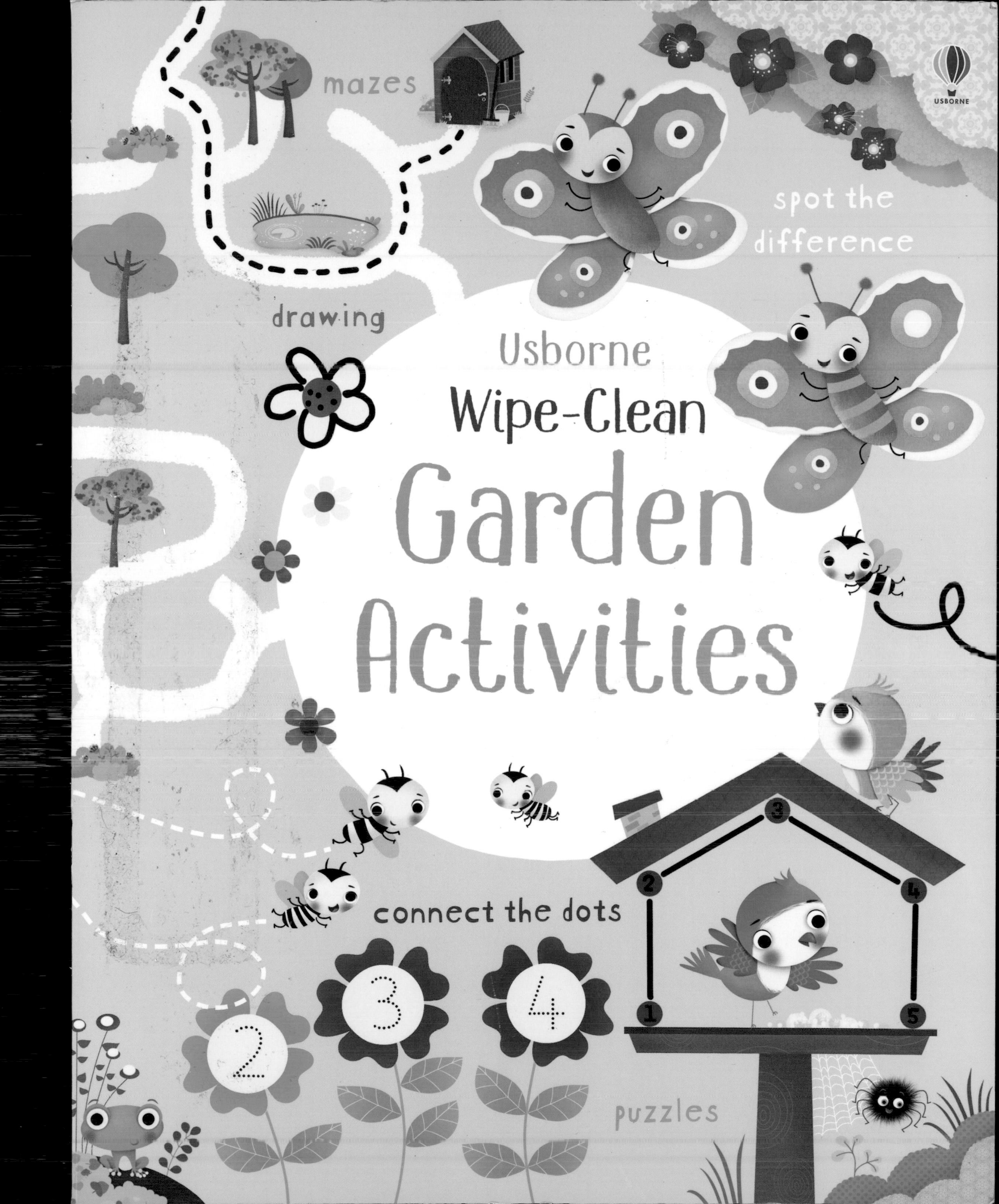
USBORNE
mazes
spot the difference
drawing
Usborne
Wipe-Clean
Garden Activities
connect the dots
puzzles

Follow the lines to see which bird will fly to the birdhouse.
5
6
7
4
8
3
1
9
2
Connect the dots to finish Becca Bear's umbrella.
Becca
Count the flowers, then trace over the numbers.
1
2
3
4
5

Count the eggs in each nest, then trace over the numbers below.

Draw lines between the birds that match each other.

Can you find and circle 4 differences between these wheelbarrows?

# In the pond

Use the pen to show Happy the way to swim through the water to his friend Hoppy.

Write an X above the dragonfly that does not match the others.

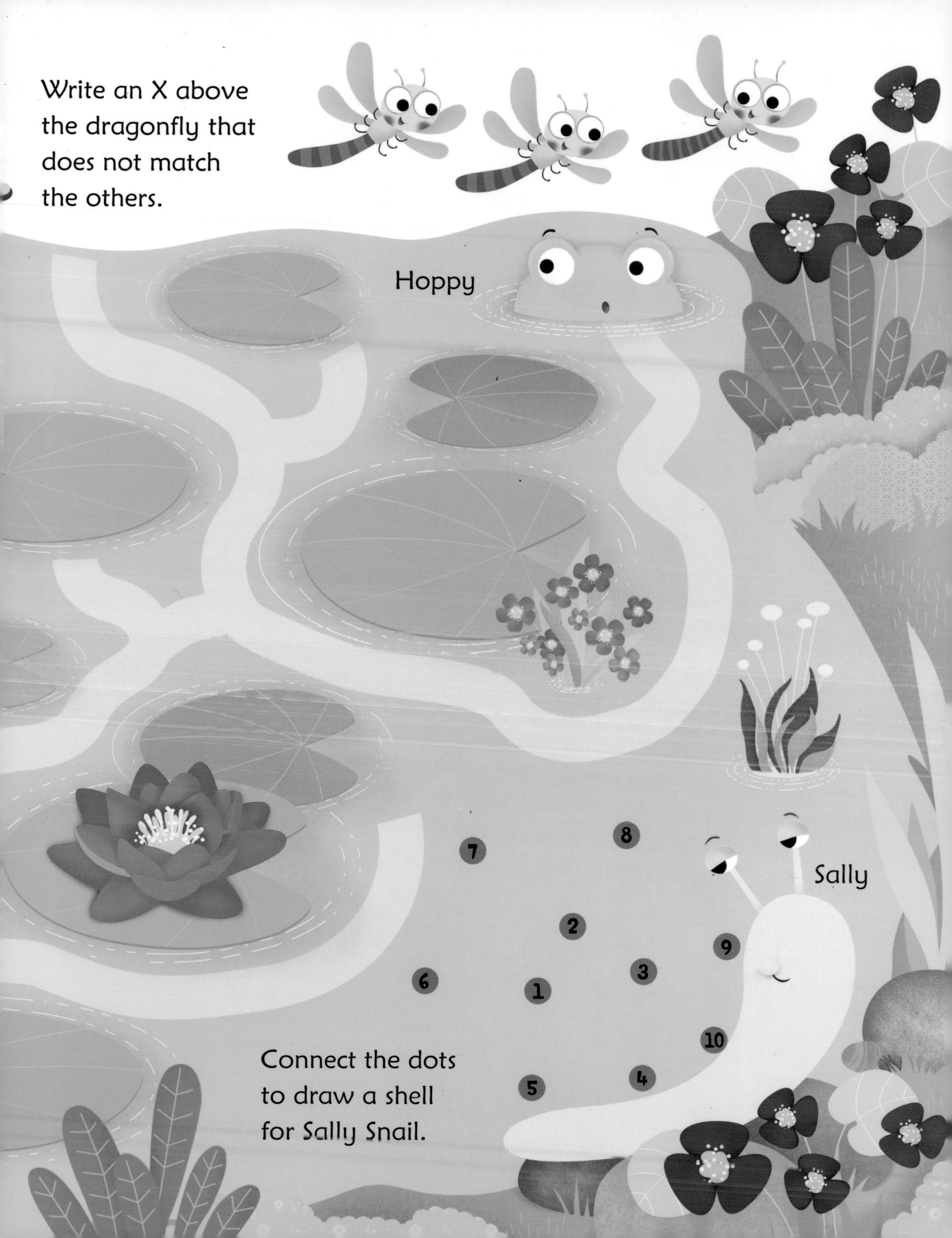


Connect the dots to draw a shell for Sally Snail.

# Summer days

Follow the lines to find out which butterfly will land on the flower.

Becca

Draw over the dots to help Becca Bear water the flowers.

Circle 5 differences between these two flowerbeds.

# The vegetable patch

Find 6 differences between Sandy and Seb scarecrow.

Draw over the dots to finish the Sun.

Draw lines between the vegetables that match each other.

Draw 5 straight lines to finish the spider's web.
Find and circle 6 spiders.
Seeds
Decorate the watering can with stripes and zigzags and finish the handles.

# Inside the shed

Draw the other half of these garden tools.

Trace over the numbers to see how many leaves each plant needs. Then, draw on the missing leaves.

Connect the dots to finish the shed.

Draw the other half of each butterfly.

Trace over the dots to finish these flowers.

Write an X above the dragonfly that does not match the others.

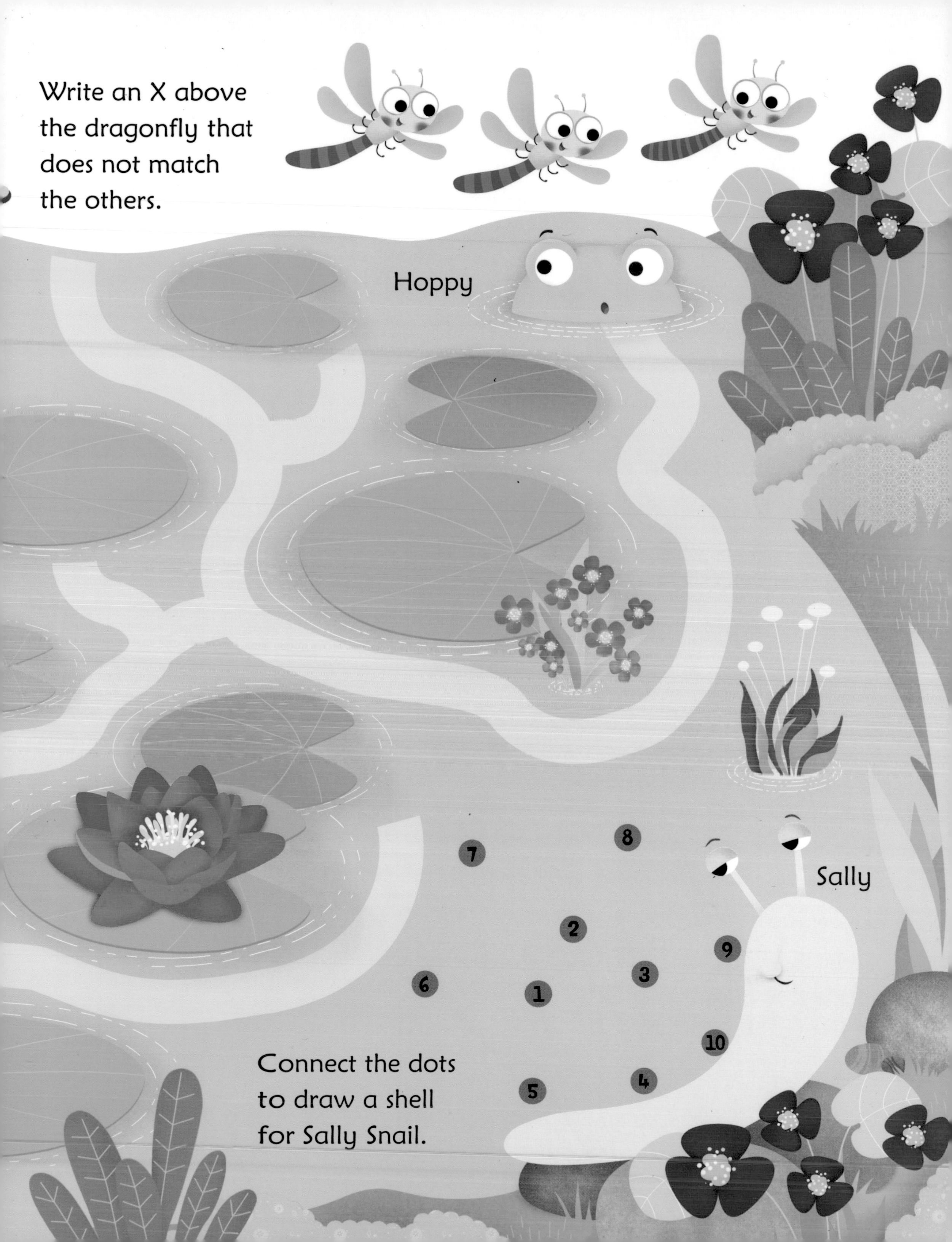


Connect the dots to draw a shell for Sally Snail.

# Summer days

Follow the lines to find out which butterfly will land on the flower.

Draw over the dots to help Becca Bear water the flowers.

Circle 5 differences between these two flowerbeds.

Connect the dots to finish
Becca Bear's greenhouse.
Draw 5 more tomatoes.
Follow the lines and see which
rabbit will eat the most plants.

# A garden party

Draw 3 more puffs of smoke above the barbecue grill.

Finish the gate by drawing over the dots.

Draw lines between the plates of food that match each other.

Draw over the dots to finish the plants. Draw more leaves so each plant has 4.

Find and circle 5 balls.

Draw the missing part of the hose, with 3 loops in it.

# In the orchard

Trace over the numbers to see how many apples each tree needs. Then, draw on the missing apples.

Use the pen to show Becca Bear the way to Felix Fox.

Draw over the dots to finish 2 trees. How many apples are on each tree?

Write an X under the bee that does not match the others.

Connect the dots to see what fruit is hanging on the branch.

# Windy days

Draw over the dots to see what is hanging on the line.

Find and circle 8 blue socks.

Count the leaves in each pile, then trace over the numbers.

Draw 10 more leaves
whirling in the wind.
Finish Dexter
Dog's swing by
drawing over
the dots.
Dexter
Follow the strings
to see who is flying
each kite.

After dark
Spot 4 differences between Ollie and Olga Owl.
Ollie
Olga
Find and circle 7 moths.
Write an X under the baby hedgehog that does not match the others.

Finish the Moon by drawing over the dots.
Draw 1 missing wing on 3 bats.
Connect the dots to finish drawing the cat.

# Playing in the snow

Draw over the dots to help Felix Fox finish his snowman.

Use the pen to show Cerys Cat which way to roll her snowball to Ricky Raccoon.

Find and circle 9 birds.

Spot 5 differences between these snowmen.
Ricky
Becca
Draw 6 more of Becca's footprints in the snow.
Draw over the dots to finish the bird table.

Usborne

Wipe-Clean

# Garden Activities

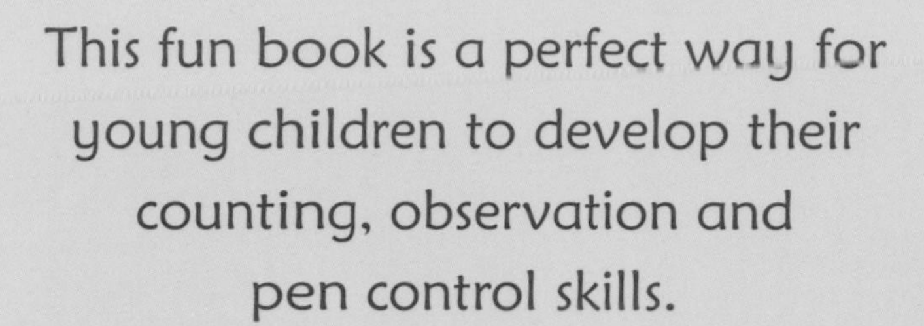

This fun book is a perfect way for young children to develop their counting, observation and pen control skills.

Educational Development Corporation

Published in the USA by EDC PUBLISHING
5402 S. 122nd E. Avenue, Tulsa, Oklahoma 74146, USA.

NOT FOR SALE OUTSIDE OF THE USA

$7.99

JFMAM JASOND/17
04035/02

Made with paper from a sustainable source.

ISBN 978-0-7945-4033-3

**⚠ WARNING:**
**CHOKING HAZARD—Small parts.**
**Not for children under 3 yrs.**

Ink from pen may not be washable.
This product conforms to ASTM D 4236

www.edcpub.com or
www.usbornebooksandmore.com

First published in 2017 by Usborne Publishing Ltd., Usborne House, 83–85 Saffron Hill, London EC1N 8RT, England. www.usborne.com
 First published in America in 2017. Printed in China.